in the snow

PEGGY COLLINS

APPLESAUCE PRESS

Kennebunkport, Maine

13-Digit ISBN: 978-1-60433-027-4
10-Digit ISBN: 1-60433-027-9

This book may be ordered by mail from the publisher.
Please include $4.50 for postage and handling.
Please support your local bookseller first!

Books published by Cider Mill Press Book Publishers are available at
special discounts for bulk purchases in the United States by corporations,
institutions, and other organizations. For more information, please contact the publisher.

for Mo, Shawn, Mom, and Dad

APPLESAUCE PRESS
is an imprint of
Cider Mill Press Book Publishers
"Where good books are ready for press"
12 Port Farm Road
Kennebunkport, Maine 04046
Visit us on the web! www.cidermillpress.com

Illustrations created with ink, gouache and sippy straw.
Editing and Art Direction by Elizabeth Encarnacion
Design by Peggy Collins
Typeset in Family Dog

Printed in Singapore
1 2 3 4 5 6 7 8 9 0
First Edition

Look out the window!

It snowed while
I was sleeping.

I want to go outside and play.

I put on my fuzzy hat,

long socks,

warm mittens,

cozy coat,

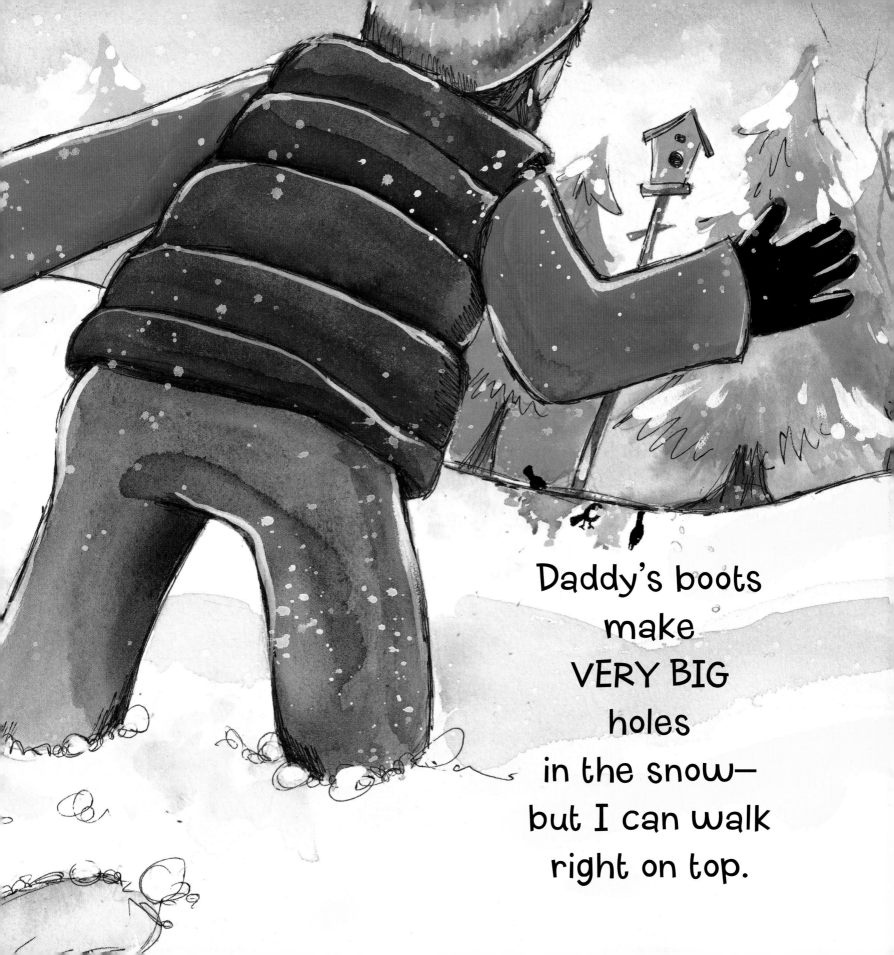

Daddy's boots
make
VERY BIG
holes
in the snow—
but I can walk
right on top.

Daddy falls down, too. He is very funny.

The snow is very cold on my nose.

Daddy gets snow all over his face. He says he is a Yeti and chases me all around the yard.

Look at all of these prints in the snow!

Daddy shows me which ones
belong to the animals that ran
away from us.

The birds look hungry.
I help daddy fill the birdfeeder
with yummy birdseed.

I think those squirrels really like the birdseed, too.

I see a bunny hopping
away from the tree.
Hey little bunny,

wait for me!

I can HOP HOP HOP, too.
That bunny is VERY fast.

While I was hopping, Daddy made an enormous snowball...

I wonder what it's for?

We get out some tools.

Daddy is
a bulldozer.

I am
a digger.

Daddy is
a crane.

We build a **GINORMOUS** snowman.
He is taller than Daddy.

I give the snowman a screwdriver and a wrench for hands,

Daddy is all tired out.
Maybe the
snowman will
play with
me now.

But he just stands there.

SILLY snowman.

I am tired now, too.
My tummy is grumbly.
My nose is runny.
And my toes are a
little bit cold.
It's time to go inside now.

Our house is warm and cuddly.

My tummy is full,
my toes are toasty,
and Daddy and I are
very,
very
sleepy.

About the Author

Peggy Collins has been illustrating for as long as she can remember, and still treasures the books she made in kindergarten. She has dabbled in all sorts of media, including sculpture, acrylic, pastel, scratchboard, and collage, though she now works primarily in gouache, pencil crayon, and ink. She has illustrated more than ten books for children, including *Shaun the Shy Shark*, *Tallula's Atishoo*, and *There's a Spider in the Bath*.

In the Snow features the same main character as her previous picture book, *In the Garden*. Both were inspired by her family's mini-adventures in their own backyard. It is always a good day to to go outside at their house—in snow, wind, rain, or sun, you can usually find them outside somewhere.

In fact, Peggy would much rather be outside playing right now, or in the studio making more books. Please visit Peggy's website at www.peggysillustration.com if you want to learn more.

About Applesauce Press

What kid doesn't love Applesauce!

Applesauce Press was created to press out the best children's books found anywhere. Like our parent company, Cider Mill Press Book Publishers, we strive to bring fine reading, information, and entertainment to kids of all ages. Between the covers of our creatively crafted books, you'll find beautiful designs, creative formats, and most of all, kid-friendly information on a variety of topics. Our Cider Mill bears fruit twice a year, publishing a new crop of titles each spring and fall.

"Where Good Books are Ready for Press"

Visit us on the web at
www.cidermillpress.com
or write to us at
12 Port Farm Road
Kennebunkport, Maine 04046